The Jungle Book

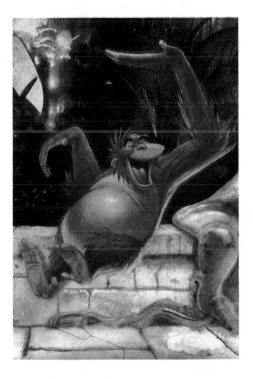

This story begins long ago, deep in the jungle.

One day, Bagheera the panther heard a strange sound coming from the river. When he went to see what it was, he found a basket in a broken little boat. Inside the basket was a tiny baby boy, crying.

"Why, it's a Man-cub," said Bagheera. "I can save it from the river, but it needs food and a mother's care. Who could do that?"

Then Bagheera remembered that there was a family of wolves nearby who had recently had a litter of cubs. He picked the basket up in his mouth and carried it to the wolves' den.

Just as Bagheera hoped, the wolves took the Man-cub in. Mother and Father Wolf loved him as if he were their own, and the boy, whom they called Mowgli, grew up safe and happy with the other cubs.

But when Mowgli was ten years old, everything changed – Shere Khan, the fierce tiger, heard about the Man-cub and came searching for him. Shere Khan hated and feared humans. He was determined to kill Mowgli.

The wolf pack held a meeting. They decided that, for his own good and for the safety of the pack, Mowgli would have to leave. Bagheera offered to take him at once to the Man-village just beyond the jungle.

Mowgli was angry and upset. "Why do I have to leave the jungle?" he asked. "I'm not afraid of the tiger," he said, "and the jungle is *my* home, too!" Bagheera tried to explain to the boy that Shere Khan would soon find him, and that neither wolves nor panthers would be strong enough to protect him. But Mowgli insisted that he could look after himself.

At last, after much argument, they set off – although the panther knew Mowgli didn't really understand. They made their way through the jungle, Mowgli riding on Bagheera's back. As darkness fell they stopped at the foot of a tall tree. "We'll spend the night here," Bagheera said, helping Mowgli climb up to a high branch. When they reached a suitable spot, Bagheera yawned and quickly fell asleep. But Mowgli sat glumly at his side.

Suddenly something slithered along the branch towards him. "What'sss thisss?" hissed Kaa the snake. "It'sss a Man-cub!" Staring into Mowgli's eyes, Kaa soon hypnotised the boy.

Kaa began to wrap himself round Mowgli's body, squeezing harder and harder. "What a deliciousss sssupper!" the snake exclaimed, opening his jaws wide.

At that moment Bagheera woke up and saw what was happening. With a swift blow from his paw, he sent the snake thudding to the ground.

"I hope that's taught you a lesson," Bagheera said to Mowgli. "You see, you can't survive alone in the jungle. In the morning you must come with me to the Man-village. But let's sleep now."

At first light Mowgli was awakened by a thundering, crashing noise. It was Colonel Hathi's troop of elephants marching through the jungle on their Dawn Patrol. Mowgli was delighted, and scrambled down to join them. He fell into line beside a baby elephant and tried to copy everything it did.

Colonel Hathi was furious when he discovered that Mowgli was marching with his herd.

"A Man-cub!" he bellowed, clasping Mowgli in his trunk and lifting him into the air. "This is treason! I'll have no Man-cubs in *my* jungle!"

Before Mowgli could explain why he was there, Bagheera bounded up beside the Colonel. "It's all right, Hathi," the panther said, "he won't be here for much longer."

"*Colonel* Hathi, if you please, sir," answered the elephant.

"*Colonel* Hathi," Bagheera went on. "The Man-cub is with me. I'm taking him to the Man-village."

"To stay?" asked the Colonel with a suspicious look. Bagheera nodded.

Mowgli wasn't at all grateful for Bagheera's help. "I don't need your protection," he shouted. "And I'm *not* going any further with you!" He grabbed hold of a nearby tree and held tight.

"You're coming with me whether you like it or not!" Bagheera said, tugging at Mowgli's clothing. But the boy wouldn't budge. "All right, have it your own way!" said Bagheera at last, and he stalked away, leaving Mowgli alone.

Mowgli wasn't by himself for long. A big, jolly bear called Baloo soon ambled by and made friends with him. "Stick with me, kid," he told Mowgli. "I'll teach you how to survive in the jungle!"

He showed Mowgli how to walk like a bear, growl like a bear, and even scratch like a bear – though Mowgli was better at tickling!

"You're *much* more fun than Bagheera!" Mowgli laughed.

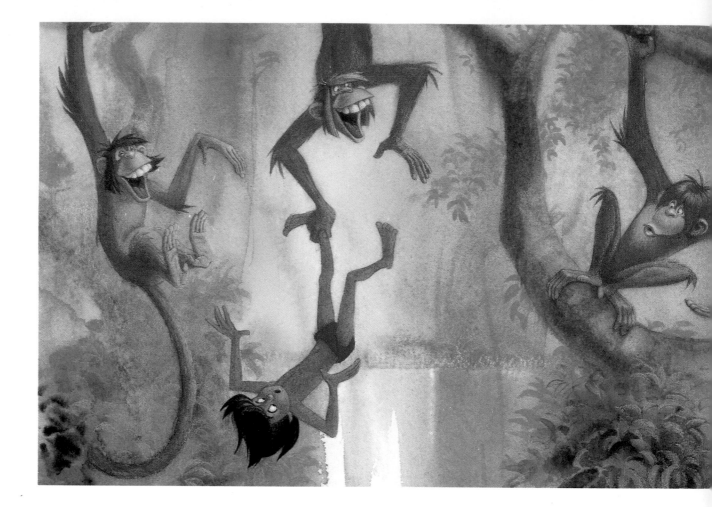

Later that afternoon Baloo and Mowgli were drifting lazily down the river. Mowgli rode on Baloo's stomach, and Baloo had closed his eyes as if about to go to sleep. Neither of them took any notice of the monkeys swinging through the branches above them.

But the monkeys were very interested in them. As Mowgli and Baloo floated past, one of the monkeys reached down and grabbed the boy's leg.

Seconds later, another monkey took Mowgli's place on top of Baloo.

"Hey, let go of me!" shouted Mowgli, as another monkey lifted him into the air.

Baloo opened his eyes at once and tossed his new passenger into the water. "Take your hands off my cub!" roared the bear, shaking his paw at the monkeys. But they just laughed at him.

"Baloo, help! They're taking me away!" Mowgli cried. But before Baloo could do anything, the monkeys pelted him with fruit and knocked him flat on his back.

The bear lay stunned for a minute. Then he shouted, "Help, Bagheera, help!"

From deep in the jungle Bagheera heard the cry and sighed. He knew they'd get into trouble sooner or later. He raced immediately to the rescue. "All right," he said to Baloo. "What happened? Where's Mowgli?"

"They ambushed me," Baloo answered indignantly. "Thousands of them I jabbed with my left, and then I swung with my right, but those mangy monkeys carried him off."

"I suspect they're taking him to their headquarters, the ancient ruins!" cried Bagheera. He shook his head in dismay. "Oh, I hate to think of what will happen when he meets that king of theirs!"

Bagheera was right. The monkeys had taken Mowgli to their leader, King Louie, whose throne was in an old ruined temple in the middle of the jungle. The Monkey King loved to sing and dance, and he soon had Mowgli joining in.

"We can be good friends, Man-cub," said King Louie, as they laughed and snapped their fingers. "I'll help you stay in the jungle if you do something for me – teach me the secret of fire. Once I know that, I can be human, like you!"

"I don't know how to make fire," said Mowgli. But King Louie didn't believe him. He picked Mowgli up and began to swing him round, faster and faster.

By this time, Baloo and Bagheera had arrived and were watching from behind a crumbling wall. "You distract King Louie," Bagheera said to Baloo, "and I'll go in and rescue Mowgli."

Using coconut shells and leaves, Baloo disguised himself as a female monkey. King Louie thought Baloo was so beautiful that he danced right over to him and left Mowgli alone – giving Bagheera the chance to snatch the boy to safety.

In his excitement, King Louie accidentally knocked down one of the columns holding up the temple.

As Baloo, Bagheera and Mowgli raced away, they heard the crash of the ruins collapsing on the monkeys.

Late that night, exhausted from the day's adventures, the three friends rested on a little island in the middle of the river. While Mowgli slept, Baloo and Bagheera talked about his future.

"The Man-cub *must* go to the Man-village," said Bagheera. "The jungle is not the place for him."

"What's wrong with the jungle?" asked Baloo. "Take a look at me. I grew up in the jungle."

"Yes, and just look at your reflection in the water," the panther said. Baloo had a black eye and was covered in bruises.

"Well, you don't look too good yourself!" said Baloo, looking down at Bagheera's scratched and bleeding paws.

Meanwhile, not far away, Shere Khan was silently stalking a deer. Suddenly the tiger was distracted by the sound of marching. He stopped and listened. It was Colonel Hathi and his Dawn Patrol.

With a swish of its tail, the deer bounded away.

"What beastly luck!" snarled Shere Khan. "Confound that ridiculous Colonel Hathi." Nevertheless, Shere Khan didn't want any trouble with the elephants, so he crouched low in the bushes and watched. Suddenly he saw Bagheera heading towards the Colonel.

"Wait! Stop!" cried Bagheera. "We need your help, Colonel Hathi. Mowgli the Man-cub is lost, and we have to find him before Shere Khan does!"

"All right," said Colonel Hathi. "I'll get my troops to start looking first thing in the morning."

Shere Khan had heard everything from his hiding place in the bushes. He licked his lips.

"Hmmm," the tiger said to himself. "The Man-cub is lost in the jungle, eh? I think I'll do everyone a good deed and find him first!" He slunk away to begin his search.

Not far away Mowgli was sitting under a tree, wondering where to go next. Kaa the snake slithered down beside him. "It'sss ssso nice to sssee you again, Man-cub!" said Kaa, pulling Mowgli up into the branches with him.

"Put me down and leave me alone!" said Mowgli.

"But I can help you ssstay in the jungle," said Kaa. "Jussst look into my eyesss and have a sssleep firssst." He stared at Mowgli, hypnotising him again with his gaze.

Suddenly Kaa felt a tug on his tail. He dropped down to find himself face to face with Shere Khan.

"Hello," purred the tiger, taking hold of the snake's neck. "I heard you talking to someone up there. It wouldn't be that lost Man-cub, would it, Kaa?"

"No," gulped Kaa. "I was just talking to – uh – myself!"

"Really?" said Shere Khan. "Well, if you do happen to see the Man-cub, you will let me know, won't you?" Kaa sighed with relief as the tiger loosened his grip.

While Kaa was talking to Shere Khan, Mowgli woke up and managed to slip away. In a nearby clearing he made friends with some scraggly-looking vultures, who couldn't seem to stop talking.

All at once Shere Khan emerged from the shadows. "Why, thank you for keeping the Man-cub here for me!" he said to the vultures.

"Run, kid, run!" the birds shouted as they frantically flew off. But Mowgli didn't move.

"Don't you know who I am?" asked Shere Khan.

"Yes," replied Mowgli, "but I'm not afraid of you!"

No one had *ever* stood up to Shere Khan like this before. It made him *very* angry. With a ferocious roar, he bared his teeth and leapt straight at Mowgli.

Suddenly Shere Khan stopped in mid-leap and crashed to the ground. Baloo was right behind him, clutching the tiger's tail!

As Shere Khan spun round to attack Baloo, Mowgli grabbed a big stick and lunged at the tiger. Shere Khan roared in anger and charged at Mowgli again, dragging Baloo behind him.

The vultures, circling overhead, saw what was happening and swooped down to rescue Mowgli. Just as they lifted him into the air, a bolt of lightning hit an old dead tree. Hissing and crackling, the tree burst into flames.

Shere Khan froze, panic-stricken. Fire was the only thing he was afraid of!

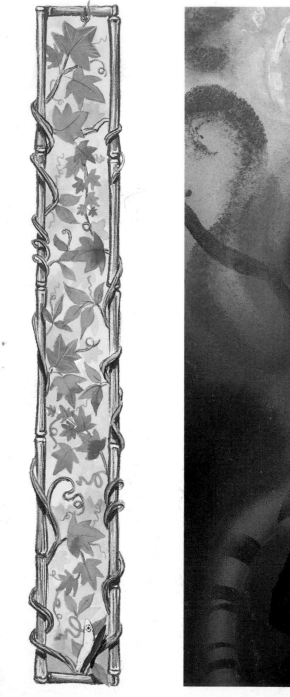

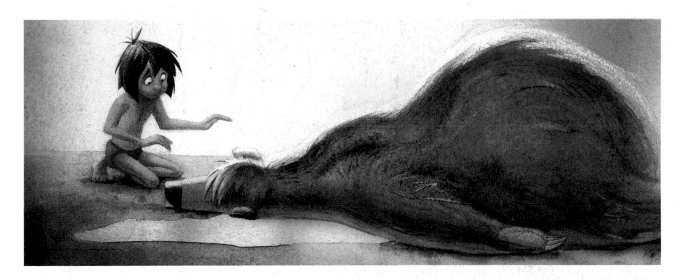

As the vultures attacked Shere Khan from the air, Mowgli picked up a burning branch and tied it to the tiger's tail. With a terrified scream, Shere Khan fled into the jungle.

Mowgli ran to Baloo, who was lying very still on the ground. "Baloo," he cried, "get up. Please get up!"

Bagheera came up behind Mowgli. "You've got to be brave, Mowgli," he said, "just like Baloo was."

"Was?" cried Mowgli. "You mean Baloo's…"

"Just fine!" said Baloo, grinning and sitting up. Mowgli laughed and gave him a joyful hug.

A short time later Baloo, Bagheera and Mowgli reached the edge of the Man-village. Suddenly they heard someone singing. It was a pretty girl, filling her water jug from the river.

"What's that?" asked Mowgli. And, as he climbed a tree to get a better view, the girl looked up and smiled at him. Mowgli smiled, too. When the girl began walking back to the village, he ran to join her.

"Mowgli!" Baloo called. But Mowgli just turned and waved to him and Bagheera, and kept going towards the village with the girl.

"Let him go," Bagheera said to Baloo. "After all, it's where he belongs."

"Yeah, I guess you're right," sighed Baloo, as they walked slowly away. "It's too bad, though. That kid would have made one swell bear!"